To Larry, for teaching us the importance of making at least one person smile every day. I love you more than Nutella.

And to Rosie and Caroline. Remember these three things and life will bring you happiness: make someone smile every day, be grateful, and don't forget to make your bed every single morning.

www.mascotbooks.com

My Hair Went on Vacation

For more information, please contact:
Mascot Books
620 Herndon Parkway, Suite 320
Herndon, VA 20170
info@mascotbooks.com

Library of Congress Control Number: 2019918337

CPSIA Code: PRT0320A
ISBN-13: 978-1-64543-281-4

Printed in the United States

My Hair Went on VACATION

Paula Quinn

illustrated by

Chiara Civati

I woke up one morning, quick out of bed,
to find curls on my pillow instead of my head.

I felt so confused by this weird situation.
My hair wasn't in its usual location!

I imagined it went
   on an amazing trip
across land, across sea—
   or on board a spaceship!
Oh where, oh where did my lovely hair go?
                    Deep in Africa, atop
                    Kilimanjaro?

MOSCOW
NEW YORK
SYDNEY
BANGKOK
SAN SALVADOR
HELSINKI
LONDON
MARRAKECH
DELHI
CUZCO

Could it be in Spain, the Alps, or even Peru?
Is it splashing with dolphins or in Timbuktu?
Maybe it packed bags and boarded a train
bound for Austin, Chicago, Seattle, or Maine.
Each night before bed it has explored a new place,
then slipped into dreamland with its tiny suitcase.

At school the kids pointed and stared—
they all said, "Look at that girl with no hair!"
I cried as I hid my bald head under my shirt.
Their words stung and my feelings were hurt.

My teacher comforted me to help my feelings subside.
I remembered mom's words, "Rosie—smile, say hello,
and don't hide."

Now when kids point and ask for an explanation,
I smile, and say, "My hair went on vacation!"

My dad says they're just curious, but
to me that's unfair!
It hurts when those kids point,
snicker, and glare.

My mom says to always be
kind and show grace.
"Show them a bald girl
with a smile on her face!"

My parents encourage me to do things that
make me proud.
I like to paint—it makes me laugh out loud.

After losing my hair, Mom and Dad saw my smile fade.
So they printed a head scarf from a painting I made!
As I put on the scarf, a delightful creation,
Confidence returned and sparked my imagination.

One day, while looking in the mirror as happy as can be,
I thought of an idea for bald kids like me.
Just like my traveling, vacationing hair,
I could send headscarves to bald kids everywhere!

So I started sending paint to kids far and wide
for them to create headscarves to wear with pride.

Bald kids need to feel self-love, not shame,
for true beauty's within, shining bright like a flame.

I've asked doctors for medicine to end my hair loss,
one safe for kids and tasty like chocolate sauce.
But there's still no cure for hair-loss disease.
My hair can fall out or grow back with ease.

But that's okay, I love me in every way,
no matter if my hair falls out or decides to stay.
My headscarf taught me that I never need to hide,
because helping others makes me feel good inside.

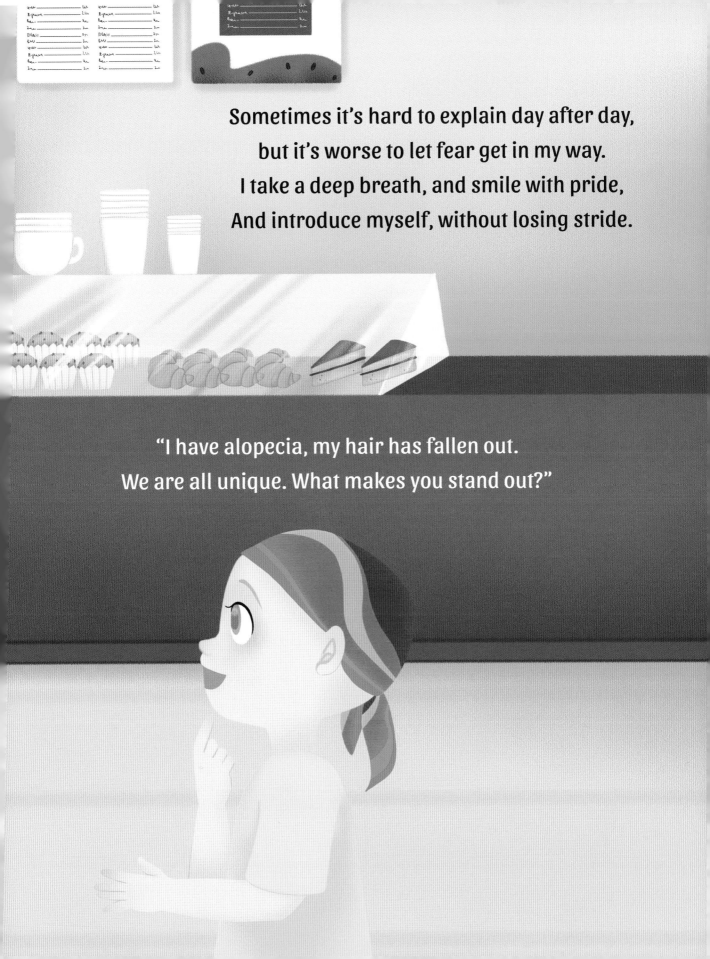

Sometimes it's hard to explain day after day,
but it's worse to let fear get in my way.
I take a deep breath, and smile with pride,
And introduce myself, without losing stride.

"I have alopecia, my hair has fallen out.
We are all unique. What makes you stand out?"

Why did this happen? I really don't know.
I was born to stand out, to shine, and glow.
This is definitely how I was meant to be.
Hair or no hair, I'm Rosie. I love me for me.

Vocabulary

Alopecia - an autoimmune disease which causes hair loss

Curious - eager to learn or know

Delightful - very pleasing, causing joy

Fade - to gradually disappear, to go away

Glare - an angry look or stare

Proud - feeling pleased, satisfied, and worthy because of something one owns or has done

Snicker - to laugh in a sly way that makes people feel sad

Subside - to become quieter or less intense

Unique - being the only one of its kind

Teacher's Guide

Early Childhood Self Portrait Activity and Social-Emotional Discussion Questions

SELF PORTRAIT

To introduce the self portrait activity, ask the students questions about Rosie, and if they have ever felt sad about themselves. Potential questions include: How did Rosie feel when she lost her hair? Have you ever felt like this? How did Rosie feel when she painted? What helps you feel better when you have a tricky feeling? What do you do to feel better when things are hard and/or life feels unfair?

Self Portraits: Drawing is an activity that might help you feel better, especially when you are drawing something that sets you apart and makes you unique. Have each student do a self portrait.

- Gather students in a circle and ask, "What makes you stand out?"
- Pass small mirrors around the circle. Encourage children to admire themselves in the mirrors before starting their drawings. Seeing themselves can help guide the conversation.

- After discussion, provide children with different art materials (colored paper, markers, crayons, colored pencils, yarn, glue) to complete their self-portraits.
- This activity can be done several times throughout the year to demonstrate progression of skills.

POST ACTIVITY QUESTIONS

- How did Rosie feel when she received the special scarf from her Mom and Dad?
- Who are the special people in your life that help you feel better?

Note: Older children can write an autobiography to go along with their self portraits.

About the Author

Paula and Rosie Quinn are the founders of Coming Up Rosies, a nonprofit dedicated to fulfilling Rosie's dream to make bald kids like her smile confidently.

At two years old, Rosie was diagnosed with alopecia universalis, an incurable autoimmune disease that results in baldness. From a young age, Rosie taught her parents how to embrace her difference by coming up with magical adventures of her hair each night before bed.

Despite Rosie's confidence, awkward questions and comments about her baldness started to bother Rosie. One day, her parents surprised her with a head scarf made from one of her paintings. Rosie immediately felt confident again, and wanted to share this feeling of pride with all bald children.

Rosie lives in Chicago with her sister Caroline, her parents Paula and Larry, and their bernedoodle, Enzo. As a family, they love to go to Cubs games, have dance parties, and cook Italian dinners at home.